KING Giggle

ORPEN PRESS

Acknowledgements

I would like to thank the Human Givens College for recognising and encouraging my creativity. I especially thank the college principal Ivan Tyrrell and Director of Studies Joe Griffin for their inspirational teaching of the most effective and transforming psychotherapy I have learned to date.

I also thank Brenda O'Hanlon, my editor, for believing in me, working so hard and doing such a wonderful job. I am sincerely grateful to Sue Saunders for sorting out the computer and being my right hand in Ireland. Without her IT expertise and patience these stories might not have reached the publisher so promptly!

Thank you to my colleague Sue Harper for listening to my first story and telling me to "go for it", and to Pat Williams, founder-director of the London College of Storytellers, for advising me to get the stories published. Thanks also to all my colleagues and friends who have encouraged me over the years.

Of course, most importantly, I thank my incredibly supportive husband Frank, who is my best friend and my stability, and who has allowed me to remain a child at heart.

And a big thank you to all the children who have inspired me, and without whom I would not have known the healing properties of these stories.

Praise for the *Brighter Little Minds* series:

"As a Human Givens psychotherapist and gifted storyteller, Pamela has a wonderful ability to transform the lives of children by using metaphor. She demonstrates these gifts in these perfect little books. No child can flourish unless the patterns of greater possibilities are first grasped in imagination. By imaginatively engaging young minds in her tales, she does a great service, not only to the children themselves but to their families and the wider community."
IVAN TYRRELL, psychotherapist, tutor and author

"These stories will entertain children, whilst helping them to access their inner strengths and creativities. These are very special stories written by a very special writer who can see into the hearts of children and help them find their special form of courage hidden in the magic of a wondrous tale."
JOE GRIFFIN, research psychologist, tutor and author

"Pamela's stories are simply delightful, and delightful because they are simple. She writes from her heart, which is big, and is an absolutely natural storyteller."
DENISE WINN, editor, *Human Givens*

"Pamela's stories are lovely, heartwarming and suitable for any audience. As well as their therapeutic value, the stories have proven to be an excellent resource for teaching."
DR WENDY SIMS-SCHOUTEN, senior lecturer for childhood degrees, University of Portsmouth

King Giggle

Written by Pamela Woodford
Illustrations by Ben White

ORPEN PRESS
Lonsdale House
Avoca Ave
Blackrock
Co. Dublin
Ireland

e-mail: info@orpenpress.com
www.orpenpress.com

© Pamela Woodford, 2013
ISBN: 978-1-871305-80-7

Printed in Northern Ireland by GPS Colour Graphics Ltd

Preface

STORIES HAVE ALWAYS BEEN a powerful way of conveying universal human dreams and dreads, of inspiring us to find strengths we didn't know we had, to overcome difficulties, and to flourish and grow.

Stories are particularly effective with children, as I know from my work as a consultant Human Givens psychotherapist over the past twelve years. During that time, I have told countless stories, many of which I made up myself, and I've found that the right story can get to the heart of the matter and bring about swift, positive change.

Children as young as five, but also adolescents and adults, have heard my stories, which have proved to be a key way of addressing imperative issues.

All the stories in the *Brighter Little Minds* series encourage the reader/listener to use their imagination in a positive way. There are also suggestions for activities that aim to further embed the learning and therapeutic metaphor contained in each book.

The story of *King Giggle* addresses such issues as: general anxiety disorder, panic attacks, developing autonomy, learning to relax, breathing to be calm and much more.

Suggestions for Activities:

Make a crown, with jokes inside the jewels. Take it in turns to wear the crown while telling a joke.

Make a jelly and watch it wobble.

Learn about butterflies and find some in your garden or in a park.

Pretend you are playing the drums and making some music.

I can remember a story that began with a magic bouncing ball. This magic bouncing ball could be big enough to sit upon, or small enough to hold. And the story goes that, if you sit down or hold on, the bouncing ball could bounce you right up to the most amazing castle that you could ever imagine.

In the castle lived a king. He was no ordinary king. First, his name was King Giggle. Have you ever heard of such a name for a king? King Giggle! But we'll find out more about that in a moment.

In other ways King Giggle was exactly like a king. He lived in a castle, just like a king; he was powerful, just like a king; he had servants to look after him, just like a king; and he ate delicious food, just like a king. In fact, he seemed to have all the things that made him just like a king.

So you might wonder what else made him no ordinary king, and it's a good thing to wonder.

Well, it was his crown. Every time he put it on his head he began to giggle! You would have thought that the weight of a crown would be enough to keep it firmly on his head. After all, the crown was made of solid gold, and was encrusted with sparkling jewels – white diamonds, green emeralds, blue sapphires and rich red rubies.

Yet, every time the King wore his crown he would giggle and laugh so much that the crown would just fall off his head. The more it fell off, the more he laughed and giggled, and the more he laughed and giggled, the more the crown fell off. And so it went on and on and on …

And now you might be wondering why the King laughed and giggled every time he put his crown on his head.

Well, this was because when he was a young prince and was learning to become a king, he sometimes had what he called his "wobbly feeling". This would happen when he had to meet with his new courtiers, those who would be teaching him in the palace or in a large new castle, or when he was being introduced to other princes that he might play with.

He would also get his wobbly feeling if he had to visit the royal dentist or doctor, or, indeed, if he needed to be tested on his growing ability to become a king.

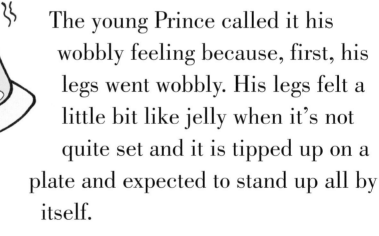

The young Prince called it his wobbly feeling because, first, his legs went wobbly. His legs felt a little bit like jelly when it's not quite set and it is tipped up on a plate and expected to stand up all by itself.

Then his tummy would have a strange churning feeling, as though a butterfly was trapped inside it, flying round and round trying to find somewhere to land.

And, to top it all, his heart would beat so fast it was almost as if he had swallowed a whole set of drums that kept thumping louder and louder. It was as if his heart wanted to be let out to play in a rock band.

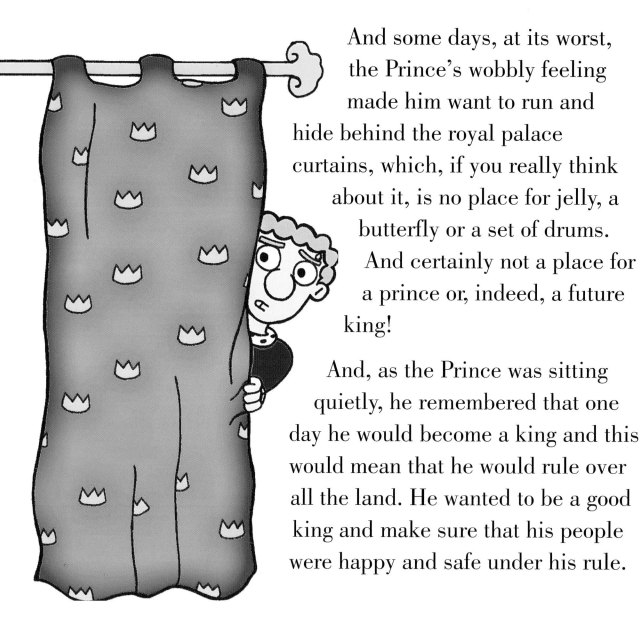

And some days, at its worst, the Prince's wobbly feeling made him want to run and hide behind the royal palace curtains, which, if you really think about it, is no place for jelly, a butterfly or a set of drums. And certainly not a place for a prince or, indeed, a future king!

And, as the Prince was sitting quietly, he remembered that one day he would become a king and this would mean that he would rule over all the land. He wanted to be a good king and make sure that his people were happy and safe under his rule.

He thought about the power and authority he would have, and the need to lead and control his subjects.

It was then the thought came to him that he should practise using his authority by speaking to his wobbly feeling in order to take control of it.

And so the Prince said in a sure and confident voice, "I will use my fighting power to rule over the wobbly feeling. Therefore I will be proud to wear my crown and my subjects will be proud of me."

He began by taking a deep breath in through his nose, just as if he was sniffing a rose.

And then he let a very slow breath out, which made a sound rather like a tyre being slowly let down.

And he did this a few times more.

And, as he continued, he began to think … just like a king.

"Jelly," he said, "will you please put yourself back in the fridge where you can cool down. Then, in a very short time, you will be set and will be able to stand up by yourself."

And so the jelly listened, and after a short time it began to settle.

"Butterfly," called the Prince gently, to make sure that he didn't startle it and make the wings flap more. "Butterfly, just imagine that you are settling safely on my hand. Then bring your wings gently together and stay perfectly still."

And so the butterfly listened, and after a short time it became still.

"Drum kit," he ordered, "all that thumping is damaging your drum heads; you need to practise beating quieter and softer, like a one and two and three and four ... until you have a gentle beat that's just like music, and then you will be free to go and play in your band."

And so the drum kit listened, and after a short time it found its freedom and went to play in a rock band.

By now, the Prince was so calm and relaxed that he gently but proudly put the crown on his head.

He felt worthy to be a king as he knew that now he was a conqueror, he was powerful and he could take control over his entire land. And the more pleased and proud he felt, the more he smiled, and the more he smiled, the more pleased and proud he felt. And the more he smiled, the more he giggled and giggled and giggled, until he giggled the crown right off of his head.

And that is how King Giggle got his name. Sometimes he only had to imagine that he was wearing his crown and he would giggle.

At other times, when King Giggle was sitting quietly in his
castle looking out at the land that belonged to him, he
would remember the story that began with a magic
bouncing ball.

THE END

KING
Giggle